Too Much Stuff!

By

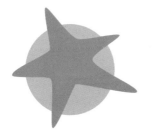

Maverick
Early Readers

'Too Much Stuff!'
An original concept by Cath Jones
© Cath Jones 2021

Illustrated by Kristen Humphrey

Published by MAVERICK ARTS PUBLISHING LTD

Studio 11, City Business Centre, 6 Brighton Road,

Horsham, West Sussex, RH13 5BB

© Maverick Arts Publishing Limited November 2021

+44 (0)1403 256941

A CIP catalogue record for this book is available at the British Library.

ISBN 978-1-84886-833-5

www.maverickbooks.co.uk

This book is rated as: Orange Band (Guided Reading)
It follows the requirements for Phase 5 phonics.
Most words are decodable, and any non-decodable words are familiar,
supported by the context and/or represented in the artwork.

Too Much Stuff!

by Cath Jones   illustrated by
Kristen Humphrey

A huge, old oak tree stood in the middle of Polton Wood. Badger's home was hidden beneath it.

All day long, Badger slept in her den.

While she slept, visitors came to the wood.

The visitors went for walks, had picnics and played games. When they went home, they left lots of stuff in the wood.

Every night, Badger picked up the stuff the visitors had left behind. She took it back to her den.

Badger never threw anything away.

"I'm sure all this stuff will be useful one day," she said.

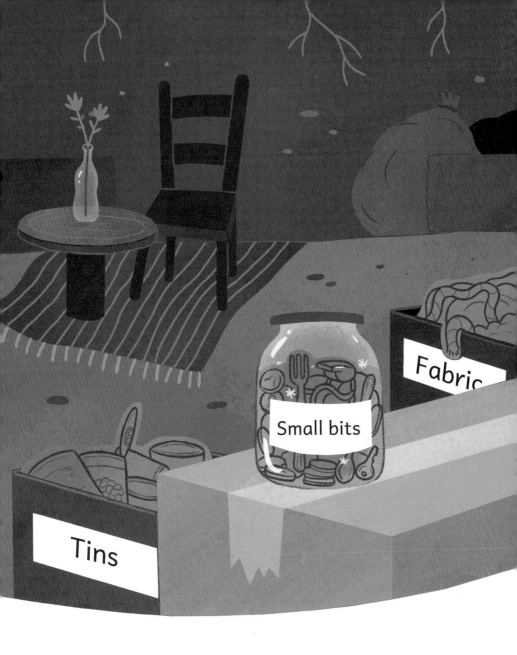

Soon, Badger's den filled up with stuff.

One night, Badger's friends arrived with a surprise feast.

"There's no room for visitors in my den," Badger said.

"You have too much stuff!" said Fox. But Badger didn't want to get rid of anything.

One day, Mouse spotted Badger sleeping outside her den.

"Why are you sleeping outside?" she asked.

"I can't get into my den," said Badger.

"It's full of stuff."

"Come and stay with me," invited Mouse.

Badger packed a bag of useful stuff,

but it wouldn't fit into the mouse hole!

Fox came to help. "My den is bigger than a mouse hole. Come and stay with me," invited Fox.

But Badger had too much stuff to fit inside Fox's den.

"Perhaps Owl can help," said Fox.

"There's plenty of room in my nesting box," said Owl.

But the nesting box was high up in a tree. "Oh dear," said Badger. "I've got too much stuff to climb up to your box."

Winter arrived in the wood.

Badger shivered. She looked at all

her friends snug in their homes.

Badger tried to clear out her den.

But it was too hard. There was too

much stuff.

Suddenly, Badger's friends arrived to help. They pushed and pulled all of Badger's stuff out of the den.

"I had no idea I had so much stuff,"

said Badger in a shocked voice.

"What can we do with it all?"

"Follow us!" squeaked Mouse.

Glass

They took Badger to a recycling centre.

"The metal will get melted down," said Mouse.

"They'll make new things out of the old metal," Fox explained.

Card

Plastic

Metal

Fabric

"Old paper will be turned into new books and boxes," hooted Owl.

"I knew my stuff would be useful one day!"
said Badger.

To say 'thank you', Badger invited
everyone back to her den for a feast.

Quiz

1. Where is Badger's home hidden?
a) Under a big box
b) Under a huge, old oak tree
c) High up in a tree

2. Who spotted Badger sleeping outside?
a) Fox
b) Owl
c) Mouse

3. Why couldn't Badger go in her friends' dens?
a) She was too tired
b) She got lost
c) She had too much stuff

4. Where do the friends take Badger?

a) To a recycling centre

b) To a park

c) To a rubbish dump

5. "Old paper will be turned into new..."

a) TVs and batteries

b) cups and bottles

c) books and boxes

Turn over for answers

Book Bands for Guided Reading

The Institute of Education book banding system is a scale of colours that reflects the various levels of reading difficulty. The bands are assigned by taking into account the content, the language style, the layout and phonics. Word, phrase and sentence level work is also taken into consideration.

Maverick Early Readers are a bright, attractive range of books covering the pink to white bands. All of these books have been book banded for guided reading to the industry standard and edited by a leading educational consultant.

To view the whole Maverick Readers scheme, visit our website at

www.maverickearlyreaders.com

Or scan the QR code above to view our scheme instantly!

Quiz Answers: 1b, 2c, 3c, 4a, 5c